The Party

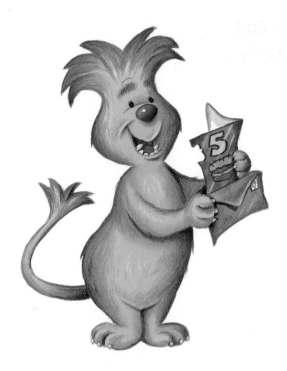

Illustrated by Richard Hoit

Rigby

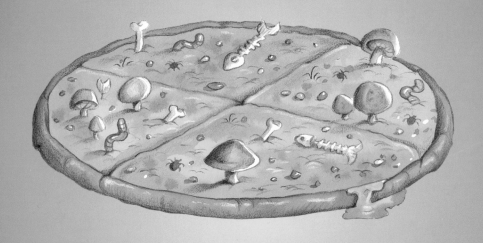

Here is the pizza.

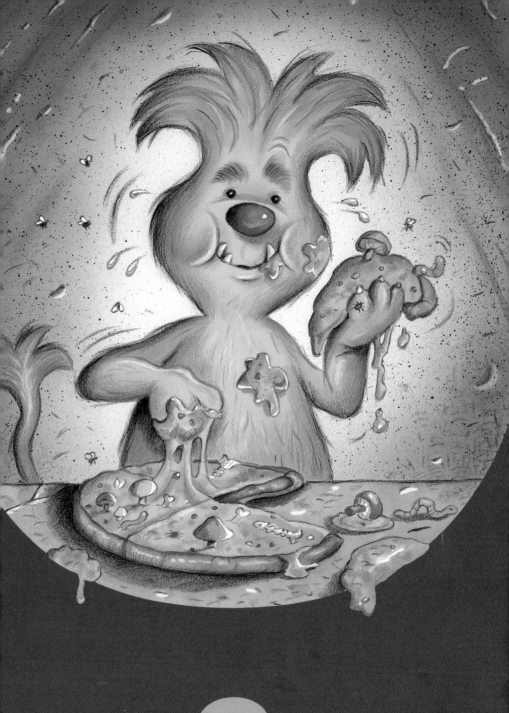

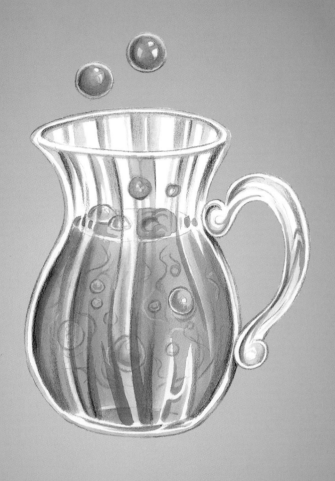

Here is the juice.

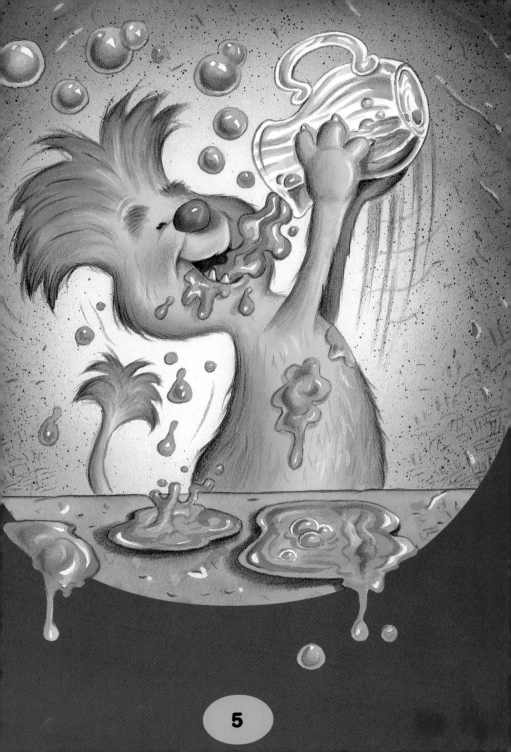

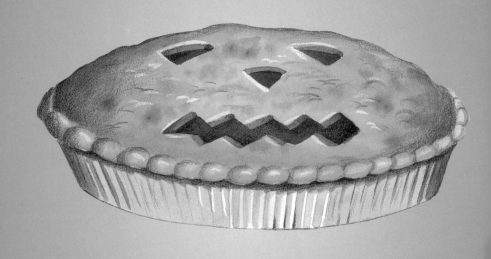

Here is the pie.

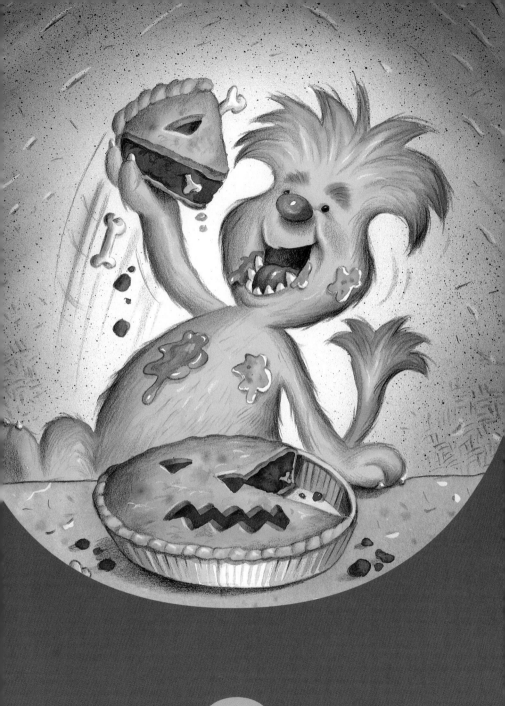

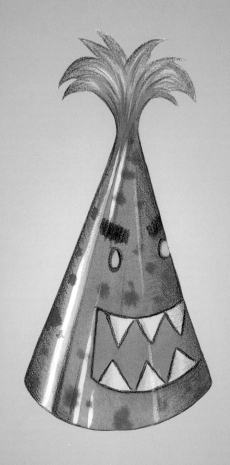

Here is the hat.

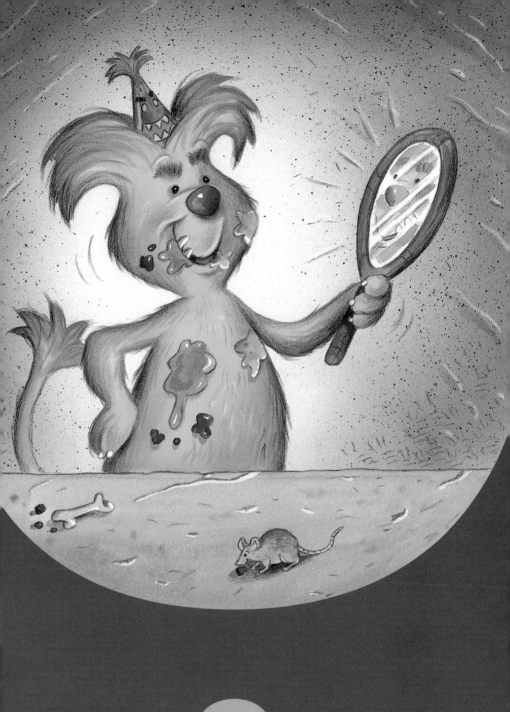

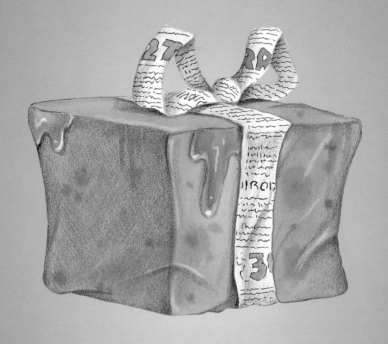

Here is the box.

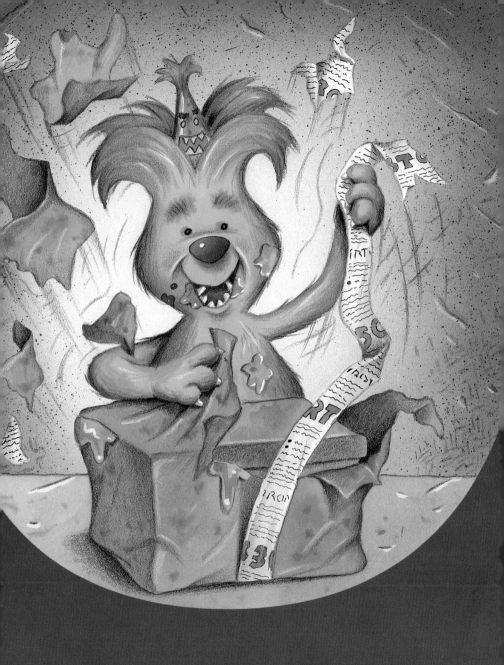

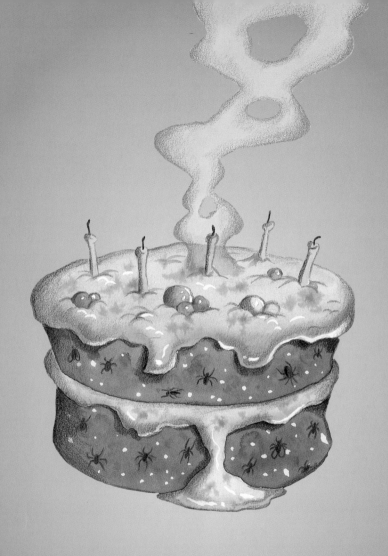

Here is the cake.

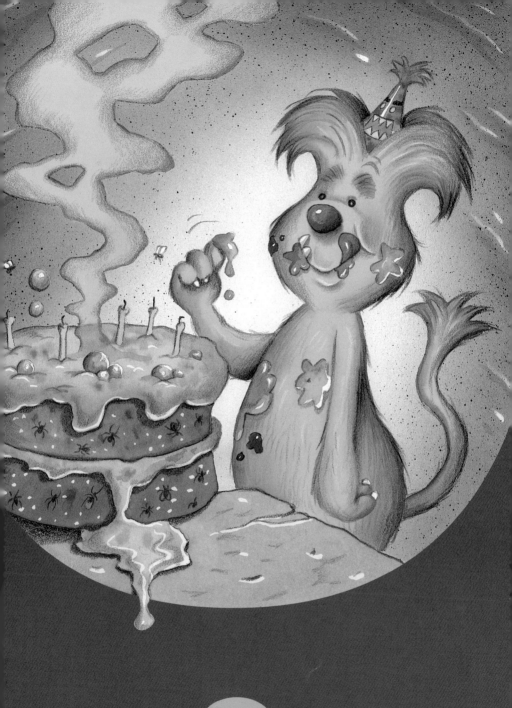

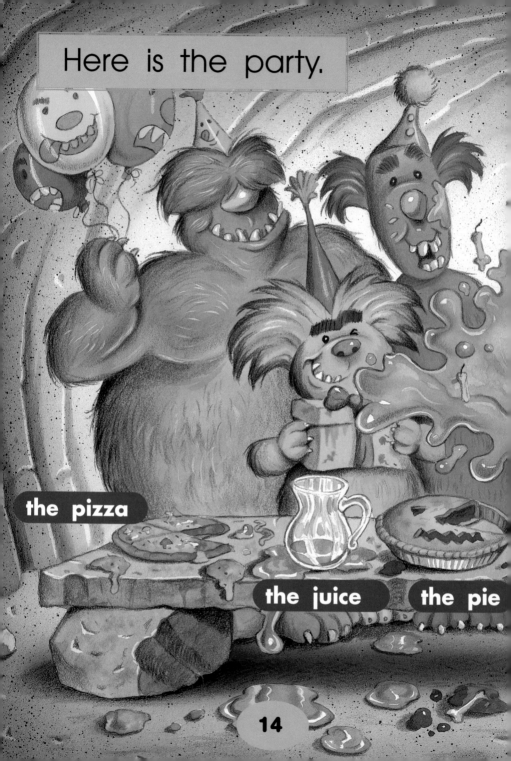

Here is the party.

the pizza

the juice

the pie

14

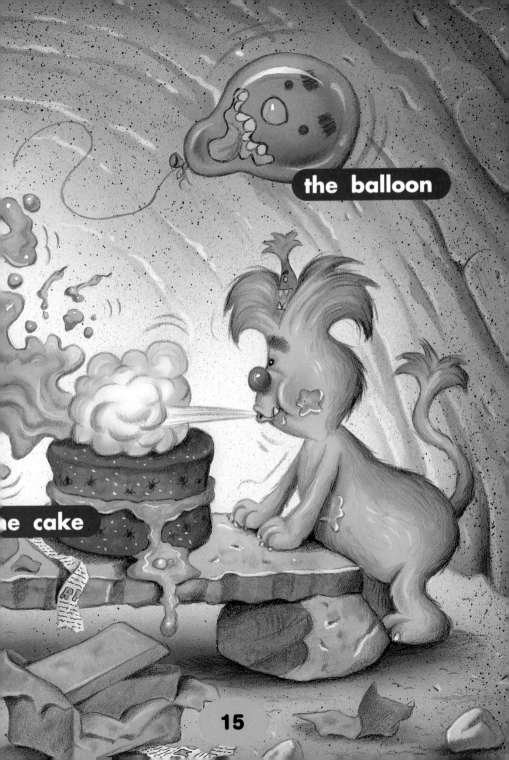

the balloon

e cake

15

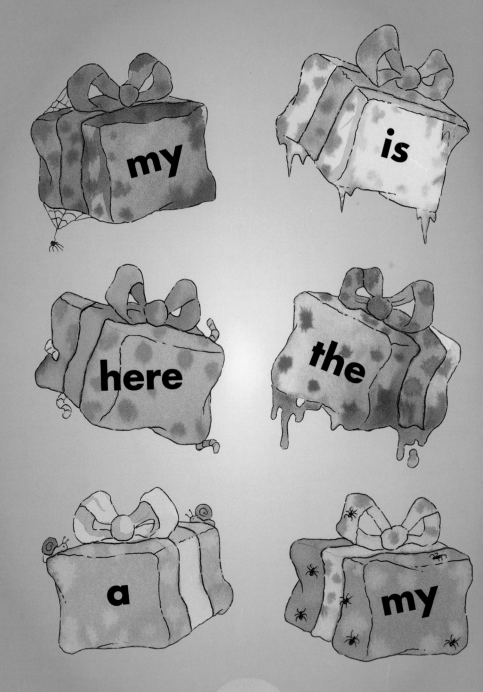